Dear Parent:

Congratulations! Your child is taking the first steps on an exciting journey. The destination? Independent reading!

STEP INTO READING® will help your child get there. The program offers five steps to reading success. Each step includes fun stories and colorful art. There are also Step into Reading Sticker Books, Step into Reading Math Readers, Step into Reading Phonics Readers, Step into Reading Write-In Readers, and Step into Reading Phonics Boxed Sets—a complete literacy program with something for every child.

Learning to Read, Step by Step!

Ready to Read   Preschool–Kindergarten
• big type and easy words • rhyme and rhythm • picture clues
For children who know the alphabet and are eager to begin reading.

Reading with Help   Preschool–Grade 1
• basic vocabulary • short sentences • simple stories
For children who recognize familiar words and sound out new words with help.

Reading on Your Own   Grades 1–3
• engaging characters • easy-to-follow plots • popular topics
For children who are ready to read on their own.

Reading Paragraphs   Grades 2–3
• challenging vocabulary • short paragraphs • exciting stories
For newly independent readers who read simple sentences with confidence.

Ready for Chapters   Grades 2–4
• chapters • longer paragraphs • full-color art
For children who want to take the plunge into chapter books but still like colorful pictures.

STEP INTO READING® is designed to give every child a successful reading experience. The grade levels are only guides. Children can progress through the steps at their own speed, developing confidence in their reading, no matter what their grade.

Remember, a lifetime love of reading starts with a single step!

For Lilly and Lucy, the sweetest sisters
—M.L.

Step into Reading, Random House, and the Random House colophon are registered trademarks of Random House, Inc.

Visit us on the Web!
StepIntoReading.com
randomhouse.com/kids

Educators and librarians, for a variety of teaching tools, visit us at RHTeachersLibrarians.com

ISBN 978-0-7364-3120-0 (trade) — ISBN 978-0-7364-8131-1 (lib. bdg.)

Printed in the United States of America   20 19 18 17 16 15

STEP INTO READING®

STEP 2

A TALE OF TWO SISTERS

By Melissa Lagonegro

Illustrated by Maria Elena Naggi, Studio IBOIX,
and the Disney Storybook Artists

Random House 🏠 New York

Princess Elsa
and Princess Anna
are sisters.

Elsa has a secret.

She has magic powers.

She can create ice.

Elsa makes a mistake.

Her magic hits Anna.

Anna is very cold.

Their parents worry.

Anna gets warm again.
She wants to be friends
with her big sister.

To keep Anna safe,

Elsa stays away.

It makes Elsa sad.

Anna and Elsa grow up.
Anna meets Prince Hans.
They fall in love.

Elsa becomes queen.

The kingdom cheers.

Anna wants
to marry Hans.
Elsa says no.
Anna and Elsa argue.
Anna pulls off
Elsa's glove.

Magic ice shoots
from Elsa's hand.

Elsa runs far away.
She does not want
her magic
to hurt anyone.

Elsa covers the land
with snow.
She makes an ice palace.

The kingdom needs Elsa
to stop the storm.
There is so much snow!
Anna must find Elsa.

Anna meets Kristoff
and his reindeer, Sven.
They help her search
for Elsa.

They meet Olaf.

He is a nice snowman.

He leads them to Elsa.

The kingdom worries
about Anna.
Hans will find her.

Anna finally finds Elsa.
She tells Elsa
to come home.

Elsa is afraid
she might hurt someone.
Anna will not listen.

Elsa grows angry.
She blasts Anna
with a bolt of ice.

Elsa makes

a giant snowman.

He chases

Anna and her friends

out of the palace.

Elsa's blast is turning
Anna to ice!
An old troll helps Anna.

He says an act
of true love
can save her.

Hans finds Elsa.
His guards
bring her home.

Hans will not kiss Anna.

He does not love her.

He just wants
to rule the kingdom.

Anna is almost frozen.

Kristoff loves Anna.

His kiss might save her.

But Elsa needs Anna's help!

Hans tries to hurt Elsa.
Anna blocks his sword
when she freezes solid.

Elsa is safe.

She cries.

She hugs Anna.

Anna starts to melt!
Her act of love
has saved their lives.

The sisters
are best friends
at last!